Cher

Cherokee is a brilliant sax player, and he's also Gene's perfect grandfather. Together they travel the world with Cherokee's band, The Calumets. Gene loves his life, but his Aunt Joan thinks he needs a sensible routine and a proper education. She wants Gene to live with her and his nerdy cousin Wesley permanently. Gene can't think of anything worse. Escape seems the only answer – but life has a lot of surprises in store for Gene.

CREINA MANSFIELD has a Master's degree in novel writing from Manchester University. She likes both dogs and cats, and fosters kittens in her spare time. She has written *My Nasty Neighbours*, a tale of warring parents and teenagers who come up with a unique solution to their problem, and its sequel *My Nutty Neighbours*. Her other books include *It Wasn't Me*, *Fairchild*, and *Snip Snip!*, a story for younger readers in which a little obsession with scissors leads to interesting situations.

Cherokee

CREINA MANSFIELD

THE O'BRIEN PRESS
DUBLIN

First published 1994 by The O'Brien Press Ltd.,
20 Victoria Road, Rathgar, Dublin 6, Ireland.
Tel: +353 1 4923333; Fax: +353 1 4922777
E-mail: books@obrien.ie
Website: www.obrien.ie
Reprinted 1995, 2001, 2002, 2006.

ISBN-10: 0-86278-368-2
ISBN-13: 978-0-86278-368-6

British Library Cataloguing-in-Publication Data
Mansfield, Creina
Cherokee
1.Jazz musicians - Juvenile fiction 2.Grandparent and child - Juvenile fiction
3.Children's stories
I. Title
823.9'14[J]

5 6 7 8 9 10
06 07 08 09 10

The O'Brien Press receives
assistance from

the arts
council
schomhairle
ealaíon

Editing, typsetting, layout, desing: The O'Brien Press Ltd.
Printing: Cox & Wyman Ltd.

CONTENTS

To my family
without whom this book would have
been finished in half the time

CHAPTER ONE

Nice and Clean

For years my Aunt Joan kept telling me that I was neglected, but I could never work out *how*. I was having a brilliant time, travelling the world with my grandfather, Cherokee, and his jazz band. I was perfectly happy, so if I was neglected it was news to me.

Aunt Joan had two main gripes. One: I wasn't clean enough; and two: my grandfather didn't give me fifty thousand rules to obey.

I don't mean that I was allowed to do just what I liked. Touring with the band required a lot of organisation, and I had to make sure that I wasn't a nuisance. That was a sort of unwritten rule I had to keep in mind all the time. I had to keep out of the way when the equipment was being set up. I had to stay quiet while Cherokee tested the sound. Important things like that. But whenever I stayed at Aunt Joan's – and I was sent there at least once a year – the rules I had to remember were things like: Clean your teeth after every meal. When doing so, squeeze the toothpaste from the end of the tube. Replace your toothbrush in the toothbrush holder with the bristles facing outwards. Rinse the sink ...

You couldn't *move* at Aunt Joan's without a rule about it, and even staying still was dangerous because she would consider you a dust trap!

Why Aunt Joan was so keen on cleanliness and tidiness was a mystery to me. Her favourite phrase was 'nice and clean'. 'Gene, is your room nice and clean?' 'Is your shirt nice and clean?' 'Are your hands nice and clean?' If she got the chance to travel to the moon, her only question would be: 'Is it nice and clean?'

Aunt Joan also felt that I should be 'kept to a sensible routine'. As far as I could make out, this meant doing the same thing at the same time every day whether it was convenient or not. She thought the fact that I went to bed at different times every evening was terrible, even though I tried to explain that with the travelling and the performing, we had to be adaptable. We would get up and go to bed at different times. We would eat at different times too. I think it's great. Every day is different. I definitely think it's worth it. I've learnt a lot by travelling around the world, and I've been to places that even older people have seen only on TV. I've also met some pretty amazing characters. I wouldn't ever want to swop my life for a quiet well-ordered existence in a 'nice and clean' house. But I was nearly forced to last summer when I was twelve years old.

Aunt Joan finally decided that I was 'in need of care and protection', so she called in the Social Services Department, hoping that they'd stop my grandfather being my guardian and turn me over to her to look after. But before I go into that, let me tell you about my grandfather.

CHAPTER TWO

Cherokee

The largest sort of saxophone is four feet six inches long. My grandfather Cherokee Crawford is just six inches taller. People smile when they see this little old man pick up a musical instrument that looks far too big for him. Cherokee smiles too, partly because he is nearly always smiling. His chubby face has deep laughter lines that never go away. But he also smiles because he knows that as soon as he begins to play the audience will realise that he and the saxophone are as one, that he can play better than anyone else alive today.

Sometimes, he makes the saxophone sound like

the deep voice of some slow thoughtful friend telling you a secret. Then he changes the mood and the saxophone sings like a bird! When the number comes to an end, people stamp and shout, calling out for more. Cherokee gives a little bow and grins, and I know he's totally happy. And I'm totally happy too to be there with my famous grandfather.

He's not big-headed though. He doesn't care about being a star. It's the music he cares about. I remember once he said to me, 'If you can find a way of earning a living doing what you want to do anyway, then you're one of the luckiest people in the world.'

When Cherokee hears the clapping, he thinks it's the music being congratulated and not just him. I have seen him a thousand times, standing at the side of the stage when another band is playing before his, and he's listening to the music, smiling and tapping his feet. He's the first to clap, and the loudest. He never thinks of other musicians as rivals. To him, they – we – all share the same enthusiasm: jazz.

When he walks into a theatre, Cherokee is immediately surrounded by a crowd. Some people want his autograph, others want advice. 'I'm wondering whether I'll get a nicer tone on my saxophone if I use a lighter reed. What do you think, Cherokee?' He'll listen carefully and give helpful advice.

He encourages anyone who wants to play a musical instrument, but he never says something is good when it's not. To him, you see, music is too important to lie about.

He's become very well-known too for doing chat shows on TV. He started off being invited to talk about his career in jazz, but he tells so many funny stories that now he's asked just because he's interesting. Last year he took part in a Cola ad – he's in an alley playing his saxophone – and since then the whole world recognises him.

'Legendary' is the word I often hear used to describe my grandfather. 'Would you please welcome the legendary Cherokee Crawford!' Thunderous applause! Then Cherokee will amble on and settle himself into a chair as if he's going to watch TV, not perform on it!

He doesn't get upset by much, which is just as well considering some of the crises that happen on tour, like wars breaking out when he's half-way through a concert. 'Keep on playing,' he said quietly once, when the sound of shells exploding in Dubrovnik momentarily stopped the music.

Not that he's keen on wars or fighting. He's full of

ideas for bringing people together, and I've never ever heard him say a hateful word against anyone. If he had his way the whole world would be one big musical group with lots of variation – gamelans in Asia, bagpipes in Scotland, harps in Ireland – all playing in total harmony.

CHAPTER THREE

Mrs Walmsley

The Social Services Department became interested in my case, or rather, turned me into a 'case', after Cherokee accidentally lost me on a Caribbean island.

I know this sounds pretty drastic, but I wasn't really *lost* – not marooned alone on a desert island like Robinson Crusoe. I was more *mislaid*.

What happened was this. Cherokee's band was providing some of the entertainment on the *QE2*. The liner anchored for a week off St Kitts in the Caribbean, and the passengers went ashore. When it was time to leave, Cherokee thought I was going back to the ship in one speedboat while he went in another. In fact, I was out fishing with Samson, the son of the local hotel owner.

Cherokee only discovered that I was missing after the *QE2* set sail. I could have been sent by boat and plane to the liner's next port of call, but since it was returning to the same island two months later, Cherokee sent a telegram to me at the hotel instead.

> Eejit! Stay put. Will collect in two
> months. Behave well. Practise.
>
>   Cherokee

I was delighted. I liked Samson a lot and every day we fished and swam in the clear blue waters of the Caribbean. And I was learning to play calypso with the local steel band, so I had a great time.

But when she heard about it, Aunt Joan saw the situation quite differently.

'Your grandfather has absolutely no sense of responsibility!' she stormed. 'Fancy losing you like that! It's appalling!'

'I wasn't lost, Auntie,' I pointed out. 'I knew where I was and so did Cherokee, so how could I be lost?'

'You were *alone* in a distant foreign land!' she yelled, almost crying with rage. My Aunt Joan is a very big woman and when she's angry, she's as fierce as the Sumo wrestlers I've seen in Japan.

'But there were lots and lots of people there. Actually, it was quite crowded at the hotel,' I told her, trying to think of something comforting to say. 'And the Caribbean is very nice and clean,' I tried.

But not even this could calm Aunt Joan down. She kept me at her house, where Mrs Walmsley, a social worker, came to interview me.

When I first saw Mrs Walmsley, I thought someone had just stolen her car or something, but I soon learnt that she always looked shocked and worried.

She started off by treating me as if I was about two and a half years old instead of twelve.

'Now then, dear. How are you feeling?' she said, sort of bending down to speak to me. I was already over five feet tall – in other words, as tall as Mrs Walmsley, so this wasn't necessary.

'All right,' I answered, shrugging. I was waiting for the trick questions.

'Nasty experience was it – in the Caribbean?' Mrs Walmsley asked sympathetically. I began to wish I hadn't worn my denim jacket and that I'd had my fringe cut. I guessed Mrs Walmsley would favour a 'short back and sides' for boys.

'Some people go there 'specially for their holidays,' I pointed out.

'Ah, but you must have felt very frightened and very alone,' she said, shaking her head.

'Not really.'

She gave up and riffled in her briefcase for a form. 'Now then, dear, you and I have to fill in a few details about you. Sit down here next to me and just answer as best you can.'

I glanced at the green form she held in her hand. 'Wouldn't it be quicker if I filled it in myself?' I asked.

She beamed. 'So you can write. Well done! But there are some rather big words on the form ...'

'My vocabulary is fairly extensive,' I told her. Just because I had moved about a lot, she thought I hadn't learnt a thing. She was forgetting that I spent all day with five grown-ups – Cherokee, the three other members of his jazz band and Paddy, the manager.

Red, the double bass player, had taught me how to read when I was six. He had trained as a teacher before deciding to make his living as a musician. Sometimes, he would give me proper lessons, teach me grammar and punctuation and so on, but he also taught me geography and history by just pointing things out while we were travelling: 'See those mountains? They're the Pennines. They run down the centre of England, like a backbone.'

I think it's easier to remember things that you've actually seen. For example, I've never done a geography project on Brazil, but I've been there, and I can tell you how hot it is, and what the coffee beans look like growing in the fields.

I wanted to explain all this to Mrs Walmsley, but she was very keen to fill in the form.

'Full name?' she asked.

'Gene Crawford. Shall I spell it?' I asked. I had been named after a great jazz drummer called Gene Krupa, and I was used to people asking me how to spell my first name. 'G as in gnome, E as in envelope, N as in nincompoop and E as in embassy. After the world-famous Gene Krupa,' I announced, staring her in the eye, knowing full well she would never have heard of him.

She hadn't. She pursed her mouth in irritation and wrote in my name carefully.

'Now – address?' she asked. 'Hmm, that's difficult. I'll put "of no fixed abode".'

I scowled. 'No fixed abode' made me sound as if I slept in a cardboard box under a railway bridge. 'I was staying at the Savoy hotel in London before I came here,' I said.

Wallaby, as I had by now christened her, ignored the hotel bit. She didn't really seem a bad sort of person, but I began to realise that it was important to find out just how much power this woman had over me.

'Date of birth?' she asked.

'The seventh of January 1981,' I answered.

'Parents?'

'No.'

She put down her pen slowly and deliberately. 'Yes, Gene, I know you're an orphan, dear, but I must know your parents' names.'

'Eithne and Clive Crawford.'

'Nationality?'

'Dad was British, Mum was Irish. I could have an Irish passport –'

'British,' said Mrs Walmsley firmly, writing it down.

'Now, brothers? No. Sisters? No.' By now Wallaby had given up asking me and was answering the questions herself.

'How about friends?' she asked brightly.

I could have mentioned Samson in the Caribbean. And then there was Victor, the son of the hotel manager at the Savoy. Also, Paddy had about a hundred nephews and nieces, and he allowed one or two of them to tour with us during their school holidays. I liked Seamus best. He was a year older than me and played the piano. He also had a great singing voice. We'd had all sorts of adventures together. I suppose he was my best friend.

Mrs Walmsley interrupted my thoughts. 'Friends, Gene?' She obviously thought I couldn't think of anybody.

'Lots,' I answered. 'Seamus, Samson –'

'That you see every day,' she butted in, knowing the answer was no. 'Now, school. Your record isn't very good, is it?'

'I usually do fine,' I answered defensively.

When we stayed long enough in one place, Cherokee would send me to school and my reading, writing and maths were at least as good as the other kids in the class. Red taught me quite a lot of maths and I had plenty of time to read while travelling in our Ford Transit van. Sometimes I knew nothing about what the class were doing in history and geography, but at other times I knew a whole lot more. And I always did brilliantly at music!

'I mean your attendance record,' said Wallaby, screwing up her face with concern. Extra worry lines criss-crossed the ones that were there already. 'How many schools have you attended? About ten? And never stayed more than half a term.'

'We *move about*,' I said, exasperated. 'That's how we live. And the law doesn't say you have to go to school. It says you have to have an education. Red's a qualified teacher. Actually I'm lucky – if I was in an ordinary class I'd get about one thirtieth of a teacher's attention. But I have a whole teacher to myself!'

There wasn't a flicker of a response from Wallaby. She just shook her head and wrote something on my form. 'Poor peer group bonding,' she said aloud.

I didn't know what it meant, but it didn't sound like good news for me.

CHAPTER FOUR

Two Families

As I sat there answering Mrs Walmsley's questions, it dawned on me that I wasn't neglected – I was spoilt! I had everything I wanted – fun, excitement, music. I had loads of people who cared for me too. In fact, I even had two families. The first was the Calumets, Cherokee's jazz band.

I'd asked Paddy a few times what year he was born but he couldn't remember. He was one of fourteen children and, he would just start saying things like, 'Well, let's see now, our Fergal was but a scrap of a baby in '38 and there was I already making my way to school with Liam and the older girls ...'

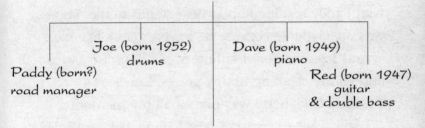

This is my first family tree

William `Cherokee' Crawford (born 1920)
saxophone and clarinet

Joe (born 1952)
drums

Dave (born 1949)
piano

Paddy (born?)
road manager

Red (born 1947)
guitar
& double bass

Gene Crawford
(born 1981) piano and clarinet

Then he'd start telling me some story about his childhood in County Kerry, and we'd never get back to the
original question.

'There's no way you could have travelled with us if
it hadn't been for Paddy,' Cherokee had often told
me.

'Why not?'

'Well, Paddy knew how to look after a baby. He's
got eight brothers and sisters younger than him, so he

knew all about bottles and nappies. None of the rest of us did. You might have been brought up on peanuts and Guinness!'

I tried to think back to being a baby, but the furthest I could get was being three or four, lying in a hotel bed with Paddy reading Rupert Bear stories to me. Rupert was my favourite because he travelled a lot like me.

And I remembered falling over on airport tarmac and Paddy cleaning up my grazed knees.

Paddy O'Flaherty was part of all my memories.

I still went to him if I was feeling sick or ill. He made me feel comfortable and safe the way I gather mothers are meant to. But then I wouldn't know about that.

This is my second family tree

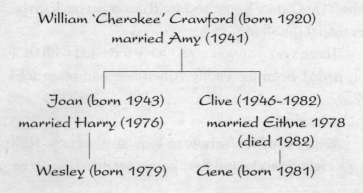

William 'Cherokee' Crawford (born 1920)
married Amy (1941)

Joan (born 1943)   Clive (1946-1982)
married Harry (1976)   married Eithne 1978
                                (died 1982)

Wesley (born 1979)   Gene (born 1981)

That's me on the bottom righthand side. You'll notice that I was born in 1981, the year before my parents, Clive and Eithne, died. My dad was a musician too. Cherokee told me that my father was becoming so good that he would soon have been the best drummer in the world. Then he was killed in an accident in the band's van. My mother was in the van too. They were coming home after a gig, back to their six-month-old baby – me.

I can't really remember them, but I know what they looked like because at 17 Zig Zag Road, where my Aunt Joan and Cousin Wesley live, there are lots of photographs of my father and even a few of my mother.

Some of the photos of my father as a boy look so much like me that it's unnerving, particularly as the boy is often standing next to a young version of Aunt Joan. It's always my father who's laughing or smiling in the photos. Aunt Joan just stares down at him, not at the camera.

'Your aunt idolised her younger brother,' Cherokee told me. 'When he died it was as if all the happiness in Joan died too.'

Since then, things had never been the same between Joan and Cherokee either. Paddy told me that the quarrel actually broke out at my parents' funeral.

In New Orleans, where a lot of great jazz comes from, funerals aren't sad, gloomy occasions. The musicians give their dead friend a great send-off. So, as everyone stood at the graveside, Cherokee took out his clarinet and began to play. He played 'But On the Third Day', which begins slowly and then gets fast and exciting. It can make you feel hopeful even at the worst moments.

Aunt Joan didn't agree. Her ears are set solid in concrete. The nearest thing to music in her life is the hum of a vacuum cleaner. She regarded the music as an insult to her dead brother's memory.

As soon as Cherokee had finished, Joan tore into him, right there at the graveside, telling him that it showed a total lack of respect to play filthy music at such a time.

Cherokee pointed out that Clive had always loved music, but Aunt Joan shouted, 'That music killed him. I'm not going to let you ruin poor Clive's baby with its vile influence.' And so began her battle to save me from the filthy music.

CHAPTER FIVE

Two Diaries

Mrs Walmsley said that I should stay at 17 Zig Zag Road until my future was decided. Zig Zag Road is in Clifftown, a little seaside resort on the east coast of England called East Anglia. Red says East Anglia is being eroded by the sea. And, as far as I was concerned, the sooner Zig Zag Road toppled into the sea, the better!

'Now, Gene, I want you to do something for me,' Wallaby said. 'I want you to write a diary.'

'Why?' I asked.

'Because I want to know how you feel about things. Share your innermost thoughts with me.' I scowled.

'You'll enjoy yourself at Zig Zag Road,' Wallaby assured me. 'You'll have someone from your own peer group to relate to.'

'Pardon me?' I asked, the way I had heard New Yorkers say it. I had no idea what she meant.

'Your cousin – Cousin Wesley. You'll have him to play with,' Wallaby explained.

'Is that the good news?' I asked. I knew I was being rude and Cherokee is very strict about politeness, so I decided I'd better stop. But really! It was an invasion of privacy. I didn't want to tell Wallaby my innermost thoughts! Maybe she'd give up the idea if I wrote utter rubbish, I thought. I imagined my X certificate horror diary:

> Dear Diary
>
> I have finished hacking up the bodies and am just starting to feed the pieces down the waste disposal unit. Phew! This is hard work. Some of these social workers are very muscular.

But in the end, I decided against this. Mrs Walmsley might just take it seriously. I could end up in a maximum security unit for disturbed boys. Instead I decided to prove to Wallaby that I had received a good education. She probably thought that all I could manage was a few scrawled, misspelt words. I would prove her wrong!

So I began in my neatest handwriting, checking spellings in the dictionary and using as many big words as I could:

DIARY

June 7th, Monday
(warm sunny day, showers imminent)

My name is Gene Crawford. I am twelve years old and I normally reside with my paternal grandfather, William 'Cherokee' Crawford. He is the leader of a jazz band called the Calumet Jazz Band. Anyone with an elementary knowledge of Red Indian history will appreciate why. My grandfather gained the nickname 'Cherokee' when he played with the legendary Duke Ellington Band which had a hit with a tune called 'Cherokee'. He's been called 'Cherokee' ever since. He's a brilliant saxophone and clarinet player and he can also play the trombone, the trumpet and the piano. In fact he can probably get an accurate note out of any musical instrument.

I hoped that the bit about 'anyone with an elementary knowledge of Red Indian history' would make Wallaby realise she didn't know everything. I bet she didn't know that a calumet was an Indian peace pipe!

Cherokee said that he called his jazz band the Calumets because he thought of musicians as ambassadors for their country. 'If people like your music, they like where you come from,' he told me. 'Jazz unites people the world over. And to be a musician you have to work together. If everybody did that, there'd be no more wars.'

When I showed Mrs Walmsley my first diary entry, she seemed surprised and asked, 'Who taught you to write, dear?'

I shrugged as if it wasn't important, but I was pleased. 'I've told you – Red, he's a teacher. And my grandfather, of course. He taught me to read music too.'

Wallaby looked at the diary again and then closed it sharply. 'It's *your* diary, Gene. It's meant to be about you, not your grandfather.' That was a stupid remark as I'd lived with my grandfather all my life and the way he was had decided the way I was.

Then she went on, 'I know these media celebrity types are different from the rest of us ...' Wallaby was being completely unfair to Cherokee. He was always talking about people working together as a team – tolerating each other, stuff like that, and here she was talking about him as if he was only interested in himself.

I felt so angry now that I *did* want to write down my innermost thoughts, just to let off steam. But I wouldn't dare let Wallaby read them. That was when I decided to write two diaries – Diary A for Mrs Walmsley and Diary B for myself.

DIARY B

June 7th, Monday

So here I am in 'nice and clean' 17 Zig Zag Road with 'nice and clean' Auntie Joan and 'nice and clean' Cousin Wesley. It's so quiet, I want to shout!! There's no music at all here – no records, no cassettes. If music comes on the TV, Aunt Joan makes Wesley turn it off. Wesley! What a nerd. He wears a suit all the time! And – get this – a red velvet waistcoat!

Aunt Joan's cooking is so awful that the Ministry of Defence ought to recruit her. They could use her rock cakes to torpedo submarines and her custard to glue aeroplane parts together. I think she uses a blow torch to cook the bacon. I wish I knew where she kept it, so

I could use it to break open one of her apple pies.

I was missing Cherokee, Paddy and the others badly. Funnily enough, keeping Diary B made me feel better.

One of the problems with super neat houses is that there are no hiding places. Aunt Joan probably had a map of where every object in the house was kept. She could even tell if the cushions were upside down! The best hiding place I could find for Diary B was the inside pocket of my jacket. I just hoped it wouldn't be found.

CHAPTER SIX

17 Zig Zag Road

Although I'd always spent part of every year with Aunt Joan, I'd never got to like life at 17 Zig Zag Road. Do you ever have a dream where you're suffocating in a long dark tunnel? You say, or try to say, 'I can't breathe, I can't breathe,' but no one listens and this dull weight presses down on you like a blanket. Yes? Well that was life at Zig Zag Road – with my Aunt Joan as the dull weight.

'Give her a chance!' Cherokee would urge me before every visit, but that was the point – *she'd* never say anything like that. 'No', 'don't' and 'stop it' were more her style.

With Cherokee if I did anything wrong, I'd apologise and then it would be forgotten, really forgotten. But with Aunt Joan it didn't make any difference whether I apologised or not, she still droned on and on and on.

Take the incident of the flying eggs, for instance. I'd gone to the fridge to pour myself a drink. I closed the door, but as I turned away, my jacket caught the lower edge of the fridge door. The door was flung open again, sort of bouncing against the wall and a dozen eggs in the top section of the fridge door went hurtling across the room. Most landed on the floor, one landed neatly on the teapot and one managed to get as far as the back door mat.

I said sorry immediately, but however many times I explained how it happened Aunt Joan behaved as if I'd deliberately thrown the eggs around the room. 'Are you sure you weren't juggling?' she kept asking. She thinks that if she's not there to stop me, I'm bound to do something dangerous and criminal. Cherokee would just have laughed.

In fact, all Aunt Joan seems to want is for everyone to be as miserable as she is. And she seems to have managed it with Wesley. He just mooches around, agreeing with everything she says. He's two years older than me, about twice my height and half my weight. His shoulders droop down as if Aunt Joan's nagging has made him start to sink quietly out of sight.

Even though I can't remember my own mum, I've seen enough of my friends' mothers to know they don't all behave like Mussolini. Seamus's mum, Paddy's sister, nags him all the time, but you can tell that she's doing it for the best.

'Ah Seamus, look at you! What a sight! Tidy yourself up my lad!' she'll say. But then she'll add something cheerful and she'll have a smile in her eyes when she's speaking, so Seamus actually seems to like her nagging.

And when I stay at his house in Kerry, I feel like one of the family if his mum starts to nag me too. But I never feel at home in Zig Zag Road ...

CHAPTER SEVEN

Misery

DIARY A

June 12th, Saturday
(clear and sunny)

I am staying here with Aunt Joan. It is very nice here. My room is very nice. Yesterday we had steamed cod and cabbage for tea. It was very nice.

DIARY B

June 12th, Saturday

The cod we had yesterday was greener than the cabbage! Wesley made a joke about it being 'the piece of cod that passeth all under-

standing'. Piece of cod, peace of God – get it?
I thought that was pretty funny, but Aunt
Joan certainly didn't. She told him he was being blasphemous and that he must set me a
good example 'because Gene usually has
only musicians to mix with'. Aunt Joan can
make 'musician' sound like something you find
blocking a drain. I know she reads Diary A
when she's dust-busting my room, so I'm
going to put her right on a few things.

DIARY A

June 14th, Monday
(dull and cloudy with occasional drizzle)

A musician's life is a very demanding one. It
requires hard work and dedication. Some
people think that a musician's work begins
when he arrives on stage, but they're wrong.
Even the best musicians have to practise
many hours a day. My grandfather, Cherokee
Crawford, practises before every performance and he's been playing for fifty years. His
fans say he has natural talent, and he does,
but that talent is developed by lots of hard
work. Furthermore, every musical instrument
is precious and must be cared for. It takes at

least a year to get a wooden clarinet to a condition where it can be played in front of an audience. When musicians are touring they have to pack and care for their own instruments. Red, our bass player, always buys two plane tickets – one for himself and one for his double bass!

DIARY B

June 14th, Monday

Aunt Joan sent me to school today with Wesley. I'd always managed to avoid this before by visiting Zig Zag Road in the school holidays. But because it's weeks until Wesley gets his summer vacation, Aunt Joan and Wallaby thoughtfully managed to make arrangements with the school authorities for me to attend – 'good for peer group bonding', I understand. I expected to be trailing about after the school's biggest drip. But I was in for a surprise.

The first surprise was his nickname. I'd imagined a few of my own and none were complimentary. But as soon as we walked into the playground a little kid came up to him and said, 'Will you help me with my maths homework, Prof?'

'Yup. Usual place,' answered Wesley.

'"Prof"? Why did he call you that?' I asked.

'It's short for professor.'

'Yeah – I guessed that. But why "professor"?'

Wesley shrugged, but I soon found out. He's brilliant! He's not just cleverer than the other kids, he's cleverer than most of the teachers! He's taken all his exams early and passed them all with top grades.

In fact, the school has a problem keeping him busy. He spends some of his time helping the little kids. He even helps with the problem kids. There's one boy called Mickey who got into a fight with the French teacher when he tried to stop him setting fire to his wooden ruler. Mickey threw his desk at the teacher! Wes is the only person who can handle him.

But Wes isn't a show-off. Everyone seems to like him, even the tough kids. He still slouches about, but it's a happier slouch than when he's at home.

Aunt Joan has never given a hint that he's clever. And she never encourages him. She'll even stop him doing homework to get on with some 'real work' like polishing a sideboard. I think she's rotten not to praise him a bit.

DIARY A

June 17th, Thursday

Yesterday I had a very enjoyable day at Wesley's school.

My cousin Wesley is extremely brainy. He is certainly the cleverest person I have met around here! I expect his mother is very proud of him and constantly encourages him with words of praise.

DIARY B

June 17th, Thursday

I've brought my clarinet with me, but every time I get ready to play, Aunt Joan finds some excuse to stop me. Yesterday she told me that I'd wake the neighbours – and it was only three o'clock in the afternoon. She also took a good look at the mouthpiece on my clarinet and said that the reed was unhygienic. 'It must be alive with germs!' she told me. 'You shouldn't keep sticking something like that in your mouth.' I pointed out that this is just what we do with toothbrushes, and they're meant to help to keep us clean, but it's not worth arguing with my Auntie Joan, she just moans about everything. In fact, I think I'll rechristen her 'Moan'.

DIARY A

June 18th, Friday

June, as everyone knows, is in SUMMER, but we at 17 Zig Zag Road are going to SPRING clean. Of course, the spring cleaning was done in spring. But now we are going to start all over again. Every curtain must be taken down and washed, every carpet rolled up and beaten. All the furniture must be moved, polished and pushed back again. Here at 17 Zig Zag Road, we spring clean in spring, summer, autumn and winter.

DIARY B

June 19th, Saturday

Help! The spring cleaning has begun! Why can't dust which has got under the carpets stay there, I want to know? It seems rather a neat place to keep it to me.

DIARY A

June 20th, Sunday

After church, my Aunt Joan kindly allowed Cousin Wesley and me to watch television. Wesley likes the game shows on satellite TV. His favourite is called 'Guess what?' People who are related — a husband and wife or mother and son, for example — come on and one has to guess what the other has decided about something, like 'Would he choose the strawberry jam with lumps in or the one without?' It's very exciting.

DIARY B

June 20th, Sunday

Am I stuck here with a lunatic or what? Wesley is the biggest drip I've ever met. What does he see in those stupid game shows? Who cares what type of jam someone likes? I hope the guy falls in a big bubbling tub of it. And there's something really weird about keeping clothes as free of creases as Wesley does. I thought he was clever! I guess he disconnects his brain when he comes home.

But I've got to admit he has got a sense of humour. When Moan brings up the flying eggs yet again: 'Be careful, Gene. Remember what you did with the eggs!' Wesley'll say something to try to get her to lighten up. 'Eggsactly' or, 'Don't crack up, Gene.' He doesn't actually manage to make Moan smile but at least she stops scowling.

'Can't she lighten up?' I complained to Wes as Moan thumped and scrubbed her way around the house. 'Lighten up' was one of Red's favourite phrases and as I said it I realised it wasn't very appropriate for Moan. She could give Hulk Hogan a run for his money.

'She gets her fun in different ways to the rest of us,' explained Wes, sounding unconvinced.

'Red says a real sense of humour is when you can laugh at yourself. He smiled for weeks after he was arrested in New York!'

'I suppose he'd never have stopped laughing if they'd put him on Death Row,' countered Wes.

'Red's got more sense of humour in his little finger than Aunt Joan's got in the whole of her ...' I trailed off, a mental picture of Moan's entire bulk would quieten anyone, but an idea had occurred to me. It was diabolical and brilliant! If I'd been in a cartoon, a lightbulb would have been flashing above my head.

'What is it?' asked Wes. 'What?'

'You know "Life's a Laf"?' I asked. Of course he did. Next to 'Guess What' it was the most moronic programme on TV. People sent in videos of things like cyclists falling into pot-holes and bridegrooms keeling over at the altar. It was presented by a grinning Liverpudlian who kept chuckling and saying, 'Ee, Life's a Laf.'

Wes said it now. 'Ee, Life's a Laf, course I know it.'

'Well, could you borrow a camcorder from somewhere?'

'No problem. The school's got one. The headmaster lent it to me last year when I was doing a project on polygonal turrets.'

'On what? No, never mind. Look, borrow the camcorder and we'll do a bit of filming. Then send it off to the programme.'

'Why?'

'Why not?' I answered evasively. I wanted to see if Moan really did have a sense of humour.

DIARY A

June 21st, Monday

There is no time to practise the clarinet at the moment because we are spring cleaning. Aunt Joan hasn't got time to cook either. We are eating quick foods and things out of the freezer.

DIARY B

June 21st, Monday

I've discovered something about Wesley that is AMAZING. It's so incredible, I can't even risk writing it here in Diary B.

CHAPTER EIGHT

The Amazing Wesley

I made my discovery about Wesley because of Moan's spring cleaning. She said that Wesley and I got in the way of her work, so we were to leave the house straight after tea.

'Can it be before tea?' I asked hopefully. Moan's meals were becoming stranger and stranger, which was really saying something.

'No,' she said firmly. 'You must have some food inside you if you're going out into the fresh air. Go for a walk along the seafront,' she told us. 'That's what I'd do if I didn't have to stay in and make things nice and clean. So eat up your porridge. It's almost defrosted.'

I didn't fancy walking along the seafront with Wesley in his suit and red velvet waistcoat, so I muttered something about going to the library. Actually I had decided to take my clarinet out with me to look for somewhere to practise.

Wesley didn't seem keen to be with me either. He mumbled his own excuse and slunk out of the house.

Ten minutes later I left too and wandered towards the seafront with my clarinet case in my hand.

It was a windy dull day. I was walking past a long row of beach huts when I heard a very familiar sound – Cherokee playing his clarinet. The Calumets were touring Germany, so I was baffled. I rushed towards the music.

There, in one of the huts, miming to a cassette tape of Cherokee's music, fingers playing on an imaginary clarinet, stood my cousin.

'Wesley!' I gasped.

He turned the cassette player off quickly, 'Please don't tell my mum, she'll mangle me if she knows I'm into music!'

To the surprise of discovering that Wesley liked music was added the shock that he thought I would sneak on him. I sat down on a rickety wooden chair while I thought of something to say.

'You like my grandfather's music,' I said. It was the wrong thing to say.

'I like *my* grandfather's music,' Wesley answered. 'Cherokee's my grandfather too.'

Wesley had a mother, but, like me, he didn't have a father. I had asked Paddy once what had happened to Uncle Harry and he simply answered, 'He jumped ship.' For ages I had this picture in my mind of Uncle Harry jumping off the *QE2*, but eventually Red explained to me that Uncle Harry had just left Moan. I didn't have to ask why. But I never realised that Wesley could need Cherokee too.

I didn't know what to say. I opened up my clarinet case and put the five pieces together. I checked the reed, put it to my lips and played. By the time I'd finished Wesley was laughing. I'd played 'I Want To Be Happy'. He obviously knew the words:

> I want to be happy
> But I can't be happy
> Till I make you happy too ...

'Could I ...?' Wesley began. He looked nervous. 'Could I try your clarinet?' he asked.

I hesitated. But not because I was being selfish. I just know how difficult it is to get a note out of a clarinet at first. It's more likely to squeak or screech.

'Please,' he begged.

'Well, okay,' I agreed. 'But don't be discouraged if you don't do it right straight away.' Cherokee often said this to me.

Wesley picked up the clarinet carefully and put the mouthpiece to his lips. A clear fresh note sounded out.

'Wesley – that's brilliant!' I gasped. 'You managed a better note than I did when I first started.'

I looked around the walls of the beach hut. One had a shelf with a cassette player and some tapes and books on it. Another was covered by a huge poster of the Calumets. Cherokee was smiling at us both.

'How did you get this place together?' I asked.

'I rent it from the Council,' Wesley answered. 'It costs me €45 a year. That's half my pocket money. They don't know I'm only fourteen.'

'You lied about your age?'

'Not exactly. When I filled in the application form I called myself "Reverend Wesley Smythe".'

I laughed. I was beginning to like Wesley.

'If Mum found out about this place, I don't know what she'd do,' said Wesley, looking concerned. His voice trailed off.

'I won't tell her,' I assured him. Then a brilliant idea

occurred to me. 'Wesley,' I said, 'would you like me to give you clarinet lessons?'

He looked stunned. 'You mean – you'd let me use your clarinet? You'd teach me to play properly?'

'I'll show you what Cherokee's shown me. We'll have to come down here, of course.' I looked around at the bleak hut. Outside, strong winds were hammering at the door. It wasn't comfortable, but somehow I liked the place.

Wesley read my thoughts. 'It's not bad,' he said. 'At least it's not nice and clean!'

CHAPTER NINE

Moan is Suspicious

Wesley and I sneaked off to the beach hut so often after that that Moan soon wanted to know where we were going.

'Just out,' we tried.

'Out *where?*' she demanded.

'Oh, we'll probably stroll along the seafront,' I said, trying to sound casual.

'There better not be anything going on, Gene,' Moan warned.

Luckily she was so distracted by her spring cleaning that we managed to get away at least once a day. I had given Wesley finger exercises for the clarinet and as a beginner he needed at least twenty minutes' practice every day. He was learning fast. He was a good pupil because he listened, but then I suppose he had had a lot of practice at that.

Plans for my revenge on Moan were coming along nicely. Wes had borrowed the camcorder from the headmaster. I suggested we get filming.

'But what are we going to film?' Wes asked. 'Mum isn't going to do a song and dance act.'

'You know those bits of film they put to music?' I asked. 'Like cats jumping trying to catch goldfish and they play "What's New Pussycat?" – that sort of thing?'

'Yeah.'

'Well, we could do that. Film your mum spring cleaning and then ...' I whistled 'Whistle While You Work'. It's a light cheerful tune, which was exactly the impression I wanted to create.

Wes looked thoughtful. 'Well, okay,' he agreed. 'It doesn't sound hilariously funny, but –'

'It's better if we film her without saying anything. A camera only makes people nervous, unless they're used to it, like Cherokee.'

'Okay,' said Wes. 'But we won't do any sneaky shots?'

'Like what?' I asked innocently.

'Like her sitting on the loo.'

I looked shocked. 'Please!' I said. 'Nothing like that. The theme will be ...' And here I managed to be truthful yet totally misleading, 'Housework, how to do it with real muscle.'

'Right, then,' said Wes. 'Let's do it!' I was satisfied. Inside my head a tune was humming and it wasn't 'Whistle While You Work'.

DIARY B

June 27th, Sunday

The filming's done. We managed to video Moan while she was scrubbing the bath, washing the wallpaper, dusting, polishing and cleaning the kitchen floor. So I've got the bit I want: there's five whole minutes of Moan down on her hands and knees cleaning those tiles — all filmed from the rear, with the emphasis on rear. The last time I saw a rear end that size it was on an endangered species in Botswana.

One day Moan called us into the kitchen for lunch.

'Don't make a mess in here,' she warned. 'I'm just about to start scrubbing the sittingroom ceiling.' But I was staring at the table with disgust.

'Someone's been sick into this mug!' I complained.

Moan tut-tutted. 'That's vegetable Mug-A-Soup,' she told me. 'It's your lunch.'

Wesley came into the kitchen and stared at his lunch with horror. I was beginning to understand why he was so thin.

'Mum's got a black belt in cooking,' he whispered. 'She can kill with a single chop.'

I grinned. 'Er – I'm not hungry. How about you, Wes?' I asked. 'Do you feel like a walk?'

There was a chip shop on the seafront called Grimaldi's where they made the best fish and chips in the world. Most of the fifteen euro Cherokee had given me was going on fish and chips to keep Wesley and me alive.

Wesley quickly agreed.

'Well, if you're going out, you won't need that thing, will you?' said Moan.

'What thing, Auntie?' I asked innocently.

'You know,' she said. 'That musical thingamajig.' And she pointed at my clarinet case. She couldn't even bring herself to say the word 'clarinet'.

DIARY A

June 29th, Tuesday

Wesley and I had another long walk today. We have decided to diet. We know Aunt Joan will be pleased because she will have more time for the summer spring cleaning. Then she might have a gap before she has to start on the autumn spring cleaning.

DIARY B

June 29th, Tuesday

Wesley and I have decided to leave my clarinet at the beach hut. That way Moan won't be able to stop us taking it out of the house. It should be safe, as there's a good lock on the hut door, but I still feel strange leaving it there. It sounds silly, but I miss it.

CHAPTER TEN

Trouble

July 1st, Thursday

I was sitting in the beach hut listening to Wesley play my clarinet when I realised that he has great talent. He was playing 'I Got Rhythm'. And he has got rhythm. His tone is great too; it reminds me of Cherokee's.

I'm beginning to understand Wes better now, like when he's watching TV. Red calls watching TV 'the best way of doing damn all ever invented' but Wes really uses his brain when he watches. There was a sitcom on about a snobbish actor living next door to a daft woman and her daughter which the *Radio Times* said 'leads to hilarious results'. Well, we'd been watching for twenty minutes without so much as a smile when Wes suddenly started to laugh really loudly.

Daughter loses her shoe – wild laughter!

Boyfriend finds shoe in rose bush – shrieks!

Then I realised what he was doing. He was imitating the canned laughter they'd recorded onto the sound track.

I started to join in.

Actor finds boyfriend holding shoe. We all fall about with hysterical laughter.

Moan poked her head in the door to see what was happening. She sniffed and said, 'I hope this is suitable viewing.'

'They're trying to make us think it's funny,' replied Wes.

Moan's head disappeared again as she went back to her scrubbing.

'I've never seen Aunt Joan laugh,' I said. 'I reckon she hasn't got a sense of humour.'

Wesley rose to his mother's defence. 'Oh yes she has! Once I planted some begonia corms upside down and she laughed for ages.'

'Boy plants begonias – with hilarious results,' I said

sarcastically. 'The BBC could make a whole series out of that!'

'Anyway, "Life's a Laf" is on tomorrow,' said Wes. 'I wonder if they'll use any of our tape?'

'What?' A chill ran through me. I'd posted a tape with just five minutes on it – five minutes of Moan's enormous bum moving, like two marmosets fighting in a sack, to the rhythm of Cherokee singing 'All That Meat And No Potatoes'.

I tried to recall why I'd done it. It was just a Laf! No, it wasn't. It was to get back at Moan. And I hadn't thought of Wesley as a friend then. I'd tricked him.

Abruptly, I changed the subject. 'Wes, where's your dad?' In all the years I'd been visiting Zig Zag Road, neither Wesley or Moan had ever mentioned him.

'Oh ...' Wesley looked sad, 'he's never had anything to do with us.'

'Why not?'

'Well, would you if you had a choice?' He had a point there.

'I would now, now I've got to know you,' I said, trying to be comforting.

'You've been coming here for twelve years,' Wesley pointed out. 'My father, wherever he is, gave it twelve months. He left Mum before their first anniversary, before I was born!'

'At least that shows it wasn't you he didn't like,' I said, but I was thinking, He's worse off than I am. My mum and dad died. They didn't *want* to leave me.

'That wasn't long before Mum's brother, your dad, was killed,' Wes added, linking in with my thoughts. 'So it was just one shock on top of another, after an unhappy childhood.' I was feeling worse and worse about 'Life's a Laf'.

'Why was her childhood unhappy? She's Cherokee's daughter, isn't she? She must have had a great time.'

'But Cherokee didn't live with Mum and your dad.'

I was startled. 'You mean he ...' the phrase 'jumped ship' came back to me, reminding me of what Wesley's father had done. 'You mean Cherokee abandoned his family? That's impossible!'

'Why?'

'Because ... because ... he wouldn't do something like that! Because he's ... "legendary".'

I thought of the last programme of 'Guess What?' we had watched. One woman had to guess what her husband wanted for Christmas. It turned out he wanted a pet alligator to live in their bungalow.

'People are weird,' I said. 'Aunt Joan probably just *told* you that Cherokee abandoned his family.'

CHAPTER ELEVEN

Life's A Laf!

'Time for "Life's a Laf",' announced Wes cheerfully the next evening. He settled down in an armchair with the contented look of someone with thirty minutes grade A entertainment ahead of him. I tried hard to look pleased. Luckily Moan was out.

Well, it is only thirty minutes, I told myself. They must have thousands of videos to choose from, the chances of them using mine are tiny.

But I knew I'd done a good job of the editing. I'd synchronised the movement of those buttocks to the music brilliantly.

To my relief the programme began with one of its

usual people falling off/breaking things features. There were some reminders of my tape. A huge granny who thought a little kiddies' swing could take her weight; a man who didn't seem to realise that if he stepped into this side of the boat then that side was going to shoot up and capsize the craft.

And then I heard the first three notes of the next piece. It was enough. My tune!

Aunt Moan's backside came into view. Wes, a look of amazement on his face, leaned forward and turned the volume up.

Grampa's gravelly voice was singing:

> Yes, I look in the pot,
> I'm fit to fight,
> 'Cos, woman, you know that mess
> ain't right ...

And all the time Moan's behind was moving across the screen. Brilliant piano, Dave, I couldn't help thinking.

The studio audience were in fits of laughter, and so was the presenter. What's the embarrassment of one person compared to the entertainment of millions?

The ads came on. Wes turned the sound down and stared accusingly at me. Neither of us was Lafing.

The front door slammed. Moan had returned.

'Wesley! Gene! In here now!'

I gulped. My guilty conscience was making me nervous, but I consoled myself with the thought that she couldn't have seen the programme. Scouring the shops for the worst-tasting food in town took time. She'd been out for hours. And nobody was going to tell her. Wes, I knew, wouldn't let on. If I apologised to him we could, well, put the incident behind us.

But one look at Moan's expression told me she already knew. She was purple with anger, hardly able to get the words out.

'I was in the High Street ...' she began, dumping her shopping bag on the table and unpacking as she spoke.

Worried though I was, I couldn't resist checking what she'd bought for us to eat.

'... when I saw a group of people ...' Tinned pilchards clattered down.

'... some of whom I know ...' A turnip rolled onto the table.

'... watching the television sets in Dixon's window ...' I stopped checking the food.

'... ten sets each showing my ... me ...'

There was no point denying it. 'But, Aunt Joan,

nobody'd recognise your ...' I said, trying to sound confident. 'There must be thousands of, well, hundreds anyway ...'

I knew I was digging a hole for myself, so I was relieved when the telephone rang. Moan just took time to snarl, 'The people in the High Street had no difficulty making an identification!' before pounding into the hall to answer the phone. 'Hello, Mrs Walmsley ...'

'Yes, I have,' fiercely.

'Yes, I am,' more fiercely.

'Yes, I certainly shall. Thank you.'

The receiver was replaced with force and Moan came striding back. 'Mrs Walmsley was *also* watching the programme.' Now that was a surprise. I'd have thought adaptations of Dickens's novels were more her taste. *Bleak House,* for instance.

I tried a little attack. 'Well, I think a social worker'd have better things to do than –'

'Gene! Stop! She is as appalled as I am. Horrified that my ... that I ...' She stopped to gather strength. 'And to involve Wesley in something like this – he would never have been so vulgar!'

I was considering saying, 'Most people can't wait to get in front of the camera,' when I remembered that she'd hardly been in front of it.

It had seemed a brilliant idea at the time, but now, looking at Moan's crumpled and flaming face, I began to reconsider.

I was a second away from apologising when she said something that changed my mind.

'Typical of *your* grandfather!' she exclaimed.

'What do you mean?' I asked.

'Well, it was him singing, wasn't it?' Of course, I'd chosen Cherokee's version of 'All That Meat And No Potatoes'. It was the best, but she made it sound as if he'd been there in the kitchen when I'd been doing the filming. I wasn't going to apologise now.

I stood glaring at her.

'You – you're all the same!'

'And you –' I thought of the worst insult that I could deliver. 'You're a tone-deaf idiot!' I yelled.

'Right,' said Moan, suddenly quiet and grim. 'Right, now you're going to do some real work, my lad. You obviously have far too much time to idle away. Follow me.'

I followed her into the garden, leaving Wes opening and shutting his mouth like a goldfish. There in front of the garden shed stood a mountain of old blackened saucepans.

'Now I want you to scrub these until they're spar-kling,' Moan instructed me.

'But how'll I do it?' I gasped.

'Plunge each one into concentrated bleach and scrub it with wire wool,' she ordered me.

'But my hands –'

'Nonsense, boy! Do a bit of work for a change. What do you think hands are for?' She held up her own pink leathery hands with fingers like uncooked sausages.

'These hands know what work is,' she said proudly as she strode away. 'And don't come in until you're finished.'

I set to work. A large bottle of extra strong bleach sat next to the saucepans. I squeezed some into a bucket. As soon as I put my hands into the bleach, they started to sting. After five minutes they were as white as chalk; after ten they were mauve. I kept on scrubbing even when my skin began to split. I was getting through the pile of saucepans more and more slowly as the bleach soaked into my fingers.

Wesley came out into the garden and picked up some wire wool.

'Wesley!' came a screech from the kitchen. 'Don't you help him. Come back in here.'

'Coming!' called Wesley dutifully, but he lingered in the garden.

'Hard luck,' he said sympathetically.

I shrugged.

'Where did this lot come from?' I said into the bucket. I was too ashamed to meet his eye. I was waiting for him to accuse me of tricking him, but he didn't.

'Wesley! Come in here instantly,' came Moan's voice.

Wesley edged towards the back door, still hesitating.

'Why do you put up with it?' I asked indignantly. 'She's mad, round the twist!'

Moan stormed out into the garden. 'Wesley, do as I say!' she shouted.

I turned one of the grimiest pots over. There was a label stuck underneath saying, 'Church's Recycling Appeal'.

'Recycling!' I said indignantly. 'Are all these things going to be recycled?' I asked. 'Melted down and recycled?'

'That's right,' said Moan. 'They're going to be recycled.'

'So they don't need cleaning!' I shouted, flinging

down the wire wool. 'They'll do that at the factory.'

My hands were stinging, my fingernails felt as if they were falling off. 'Well, you know where you can stick your pots!' I shouted.

Then I ran!

CHAPTER TWELVE

Destruction

I ran out of the house, horrified at what I had done. When Cherokee heard about it, I would be in real trouble. Moan was wrong in thinking that Cherokee allowed me to behave any way I wanted. He insisted on politeness and he was always telling me that my Aunt Joan was a good woman. He wouldn't punish me but when you live with someone like Cherokee, just knowing he's disappointed with you is punishment enough.

I slowed down as I passed Grimaldi's. When I reached the seafront, I breathed in the ozone-filled air. It made me feel better. The sea was washing fiercely against the sea wall, spraying me as I passed.

I shivered. It was quite cold for July. I wished I'd stopped long enough to grab my jacket.

I headed for Wesley's hideaway. The line of beach huts stretched in front of me, but one door was open, hammering against the side of the hut in the wind.

I recognised the yellow painted floor of Wesley's hut and began running again. He never left his hut unlocked, there were too many valuables inside. *My* clarinet was inside!

I reached the hut and stared in disbelief at the devastation. A heap of tangled tapes lay on the floor. Each cassette had been pulled from its holder and then twisted and snapped; books were torn from their covers. The wooden chairs were no more than firewood. And my beloved clarinet had been crushed and mutilated; each piece had been ground into the floor.

Nothing had been taken; everything had been destroyed.

How could anyone could do such a thing?

Then a chilling thought came to me: Moan had done this! And I began to run once more – back to Zig Zag Road as if Wesley's life depended on it.

CHAPTER THIRTEEN

Discovery

J'm not sure what I expected to find back at 17 Zig Zag Road. But I came through the back door into an eerie quiet. Then I heard an unfamiliar sound. Wesley's voice was raised in anger.

'Mum, you can't read that! It's Gene's private diary!'

I felt grateful to Wes, although I was surprised. Surely he realised his mum sneaked a look at Diary A whenever she checked my room for dust particles.

Then I went cold with fear – supposing she was reading Diary B, not Diary A? My jacket was hanging in the hall. I checked the concealed inner pocket. Diary B was gone!

All those remarks I'd made about Moan! 'Moan' – how could I explain that away? I was in big trouble.

I rushed into the sittingroom. Moan and Wallaby were standing there like two finalists in a Purse Your Lips competition.

Moan was holding Diary B. 'This proves he's been determined to cause trouble from the start,' she was complaining to the social worker.

'Certainly sending that video was a shocking thing to do,' agreed Wallaby.

'It sort of got out of hand,' I explained, looking at Wes. If I should apologise to anyone, I thought, it was to him. Until I knew he wasn't angry about 'Life's a L a f ', I couldn't bear to tell him about the beach hut.

He gave me a look back that was half smile, half wonderment. 'That was an incredible clarinet solo,' he said, 'sort of wailing. How does he do it?'

I grinned. He was talking about Cherokee's solo in 'All That Meat And No Potatoes'. With Wes, the music came first now.

'You should hear him in "If I Had You",' I answered. 'That's –'

'This is what I have to put up with!' snapped Moan to Wallaby. 'This sort of talk! And such ingratitude!'

But Wallaby had seen a ray of hope. 'Well, Joan,

there does seem to be signs of positive peer group bonding here,' she said. 'That second diary shows it too. And it also reveals a developing sense of personal identity.'

This didn't suit Moan, 'But sending that video shows the boy's been influenced in a most unsavoury way. He is quite wild.'

Wild! She was calling me wild after what she'd done to the beach hut?

Mrs Walmsley's face was a mass of worry lines. 'Well, we must certainly review his position. May I see that?' Moan handed Diary B over as if it was an explosive device.

'Let me see ...' She read out my entry for July 9th.

> I'm beginning to wonder where all this will end. Although it's fun here with Wes, I don't want to miss the Calumets' tour of Ireland. Cherokee's playing in Dublin and then he said we'd have time for a fishing holiday in Dingle with Seamus.
>
> PS Remember to practise 'Danny Boy'.

'Well, we can't have that,' said Wallaby decisively. 'In the circumstances it would be better if you stayed here.'

'What circumstances?' I yelled. It didn't make any sense. She knew Zig Zag Road was driving me crazy so she was making me stay there longer.

Moan scowled. 'All this galavanting in foreign countries has got to stop,' she added.

'Quite right,' agreed Wallaby. 'Stay here where you are safe. Then we'll see about organising a sensible lifestyle for you.'

'Sensible lifestyle' – the words sounded like a prison sentence.

CHAPTER FOURTEEN

Prisoner

Moan began behaving like a prison warder as soon as Wallaby left. 'I'm not letting you out of my sight,' she threatened. 'You'll be off doing something silly if I don't do my duty.'

Being imprisoned without trial, I had plenty of time for my diary. Diary B, that is. There didn't seem much point writing Diary A any more, although Wallaby had returned both. 'They are, after all, your own personal property,' she'd told me, through tight lips.

'So was my clarinet,' I could have said, but it wouldn't have done any good. People like Mrs Walmsley and Moan are only fair about *trivial* matters.

DIARY B

July 7th, Wednesday
(view of weather conditions
obstructed by prison bars)

J know what it's like to be related to someone
famous. Soon, J'm going to know what it's like
to be related to someone notorious. The tab-
loids will probably hound me for my story as
the nephew of the woman who massacred the
entire population of Clifftown. Anybody who
can break open a beach hut, smash a valuable
clarinet and then go berserk with someone
else's music collection is capable of anything.
Moan'll stride out onto the pier and blast them
all. The terminator in a floral apron. 'Hasta
La Vista, baby!'

It wasn't until a few hours later that I had a chance to
speak to Wes. Moan was in the garden venting her anger by scrubbing out a dustbin. I was trying to creep
up on the subject of the beach hut. It isn't easy giving
bad news.

'She's really gone too far this time,' I said.

'I know. She just can't see she's never going to con-
trol you like she does the dust!' Wes turned to me.
'You realise it's a neurotic condition?'

'What is?'

'All this cleaning. What she doesn't understand, she sweeps away.'

'Well, she can sweep me away any time she likes. I want to get out of here!' But it was hopeless. As usual Cherokee had left no address. I knew he was touring Germany, but that was all.

'I can understand that,' said Wes thoughtfully. But I hardly noticed. I was angry.

'She's completely round the bend, you realise that?' I went on, warming to my subject. 'She's a few sandwiches short of a picnic.'

'A few connections short of a full circuit?' suggested Wes, getting the idea.

'Not playing with a full pack of cards,' I continued. 'I mean, look what she did to your beach hut! Was that the behaviour of a sane person?' I asked.

A look of horror spread over Wes's face. 'What did you say?' he asked slowly.

'She's been to the beach hut,' I told him. 'She must have been watching us. She followed us down to the seafront, saw your hut and returned later to destroy everything.'

'Everything? Your clarinet?'

'Everything.'

CHAPTER FIFTEEN

A Turning Point

Wesley sat quite still. I kept on talking because I couldn't bear the silence. 'The clarinet's in bits,' I told him, 'and sort of mangled.'

He shook his head in disbelief. Just then Moan came in from the garden. She was wiping her hands dry from scrubbing out the dustbin. They were large strong hands, powerful hands. Wesley stared at them as if he was seeing them for the first time.

'What are you two up to?' asked Moan.

I thought indignantly of the lies she had told about Cherokee. How she had told Wes he'd jumped ship. She made me so angry!

Cherokee was fond of quoting some poet who said that music had 'Charms to soothe the savage breast'. Well, I felt extremely savage at that moment. I wanted to grab hold of my clarinet and play a few numbers that would make me feel less angry. But of course I couldn't. The only clarinet in the neighbourhood was now a mass of mangled wood. And I couldn't even listen to music at 17 Zig Zag Road. The only sounds were of Moan thumping her way around the house and nagging me. She'd banned me from leaving the house. She would have liked to keep Wesley in as well, but he had to go to school, he had exams coming up. He sneaked out the next morning without saying a word to either of us.

DIARY B

July 15th, Thursday

How can anyone as clever as Wesley be taken in by this idea that Moan is good? I know Cherokee believes it too, but that's un-derstandable because he rarely sees her. A quick 'hello' on the doorstep when he's leaving me at Zig Zag Road and he's off.

She's managed to brain-wash everyone with this idea that she's good. It's a wonder she hasn't tried to extract our brains and put them in the washing machine, just to make sure they're 'nice and clean'.

I'm going to write Diary A too, but now Moan and Mrs Walmsley will have to recognise it for what it is —what I am supposed to think.

DIARY A

July 15th, Thursday

Because they are concerned about my welfare, my Aunt Joan and Mrs Walmsley are keeping me away from everything I like and enjoy — the Calumets, my clarinet, music, Cherokee. I am very fortunate to have two such good people dedicated to worrying about me all the time.

I'm worried about Wesley. I keep picturing the beach hut and I know how he must feel about it. But he hasn't mentioned it to me again nor said a word to Moan.

Since I think Moan deserves to be sliced into pieces as thin as clarinet reed, then stuffed down a tuba, I'm a bit worried. If Wes is thinking the same way, what's he going to do next?

CHAPTER SIXTEEN

Escape

J knew as soon as Wes walked through the door that he'd been planning something.

He came in as quietly as ever, shutting the door gently behind him and saying simply, 'It's me.' But something had changed in him. Gone was that shocked, hurt expression that he'd worn since he learnt about the beach hut. There was an almost-smile on his face and he looked quietly pleased with himself.

Moan sensed it too. 'Why are you grinning like that?' she asked.

'No reason,' answered Wesley, walking stiffly round the kitchen. Then he did something quite amazing – he started whistling! He began very softly, but even so Moan jumped back in surprise and I just stared at him in wonder. If he had strangled Moan with a piano wire, I wouldn't have been more amazed. And still he went on whistling.

I soon recognised the tune – 'When Irish Eyes Are Smiling.' It was a clue. Somehow, Wes was making sure that I would get to Ireland. Luckily Moan couldn't possibly guess what was going on because she'd never listened to any music.

I kept close to Wes after that but so did Moan, so the three of us followed each other around the small house.

Still smiling, Wesley sat down and turned the television on. I sat down.

Moan sat down between us.

'And now,' came a wildly excited voice from the television. 'It's *"Top of the Pops"!'*

'Turn that nonsense off!' ordered Moan.

Wesley rose slowly and turned the television set off. He stood by the window and stared out through the dazzling white net curtains. I went and stood next to him. He turned towards me, about to speak, but as he opened his mouth, Moan shoved herself in between us.

The house seemed to have shrunk. Wherever I was, there was Moan. I'm sure that if I'd sat in the airing cupboard, she would have too. And all the time, Wesley was trying to tell me something ...

Moan didn't dare leave us to go shopping, so we sat down to a meal of left-overs.

'There's some of last Friday's battered plaice, beetroot and cold custard,' Moan announced, sawing the custard into three thick slices.

In more cheerful times I might have risked a joke about the plaice, but not now. The three of us sat dumbly, until the cheerful sound of Wesley's whistling broke the silence.

Even I was surprised at him whistling while eating. After all, you don't want bits of beetroot shooting over the table, do you? Wesley wasn't just trying to annoy Moan or take his mind off the cold fish and beetroot. He was sending me another message. I heard two lines of 'Button Up Your Overcoat' before Moan snapped 'Quiet!'

I grinned. I didn't mind Moan now. I wasn't going to have to listen to her much longer. Wesley was telling me that it was time to get my things and go.

I asked for permission to leave the table and went upstairs. I looked at my possessions spread around the guest bedroom – clothes, a few books, a football – none of these was worth taking with me.

One thing that travelling teaches you is that everyday possessions aren't very important. When you're in Rome and your suitcases have been sent to New York by mistake, you have to do without them and start again. And it's not so difficult to do.

I had only one object with me that I valued – my clarinet. Moan had destroyed that and she was welcome to everything else.

I bounded down the stairs into the kitchen where Wesley was making a cup of tea.

'What have you been up to?' Moan asked suspiciously.

'Getting ready – for bed,' I answered.

'It's only six thirty!'

I yawned. 'I feel whacked,' I explained.

Moan gave me a searching look. 'You're up to something, Gene, but mark my words it won't work.'

I nodded at her as if I was listening. In fact, I was listening carefully to Wesley. He was whistling again and I recognised the tune immediately. 'April In Paris', a very beautiful tune too, but what was Wesley trying to tell me? Surely Cherokee didn't expect me to get to Paris by myself. If he did, then I'd have a go, but since he had my passport and I had only € 2.72 in my pocket, it would be a bit tough. And it was only July, April seemed a long way off.

Then I got it! The song goes like this:

> April in Paris,
> Chestnuts in blossom
> Holiday tables under the trees ...

Well, Grimaldi's has tables outside where people sit and eat fish and chips. These tables are under some chestnut trees. I knew that Grampa Cherokee would be waiting for me there. I leapt up. 'Thanks, Wes!' I called as I sped out of the kitchen.

Moan lunged at me, grabbing my T-shirt. 'Where are you going?'

I pulled free. I didn't have a second to spare. I rushed towards the door with Moan still shouting, 'Where are you going?'

'Ireland!' I called back over my shoulder, as I ran away down Zig Zag Road.

CHAPTER SEVENTEEN

The Getaway

I pounded towards the seafront and Grimaldi's even faster this time. Sure enough, sitting under a chestnut tree was the unmistakable figure of Cherokee.

I sprinted towards him.

'Gene!' he cried. 'Thank goodness you're all right! Wesley said it was an emergency.'

'It is! Quick, Grampa. Moan might be right behind us!'

We ran towards the Ford Transit van that had 'The Calumet Jazz Band' written in letters a metre high along its side.

I groaned. 'It'll be difficult *not* to recognise us, won't it? Moan will spot us immediately!'

'No time for disguises,' Grampa said, panting slightly as he started the van. 'Wesley was lucky to catch me this morning. We only got back from Germany last night. I drove straight here.'

'Moan's given us a terrible time!' I complained.

He looked baffled. 'Moan? Oh I see – your Auntie Joan. Now listen, Gene, your Aunt Joan is –'

'Yes, I know,' I interrupted, 'my Aunt Joan is a very good woman, but if we don't get away fast, dear Auntie Joan might descend upon us and tear us limb from limb – for our own good, of course!' Even though I wanted to get away more than anything, I half expected Cherokee to stop me, or at least to say we'd got to clear it with Moan first. But he didn't.

We sped away from Clifftown, away from Moan.

'Where're the Calumets?' I asked.

'They've gone to Shrewsbury. We'll meet them there.'

'How did the tour go?'

'Fine! Red's a bit miserable.'

'Why?'

'He met a girl in Mannheim. It's true love. He's starting to learn German!'

All across England we chatted about my family, Red, Dave, Paddy and Joe. However tired they were, I knew they'd make a fuss of me when we got to the hotel. And not once did Cherokee ask me why I'd run away.

We were racing along a motorway somewhere in the middle of England in a Ford Transit van, and yet all I could think was, 'Great! I'm home!'

CHAPTER EIGHTEEN

The Journey

Next day, we headed for the ferry at Holyhead, and Ireland. The idea that Moan or Mrs Walmsley might be following had never left me. I wished too that I had snatched up a photograph of my parents before leaving 17 Zig Zag Road, hopefully for the last time.

Paddy drove the Ford Transit van and, as he drove, he sang all the Irish songs he knew. He had a terrible voice as Dave and Joe kept telling him.

'You're in the wrong key, you silly idiot!'

'He's not in any key! That's not music – that's environmental pollution.'

'Sure all the O'Flahertys are musical,' he assured us. 'It comes as easy to us as breathing. Young Seamus has passed his Grade 7 with distinction. And he's singing at the Galway Festival.'

'That's your nephew not you, you eejit!' laughed Joe. 'And what d'you mean, "as easy as breathing"? You're asthmatic!'

But the more he was insulted, the louder Paddy sang and the more cheerful I became. I was used to the Calumets and all the arguments they had – the serious as well as the friendly sort. It all added up to a happier atmosphere than the one I'd left behind at Zig Zag Road. The thought that I might be forced to return there until I was sixteen was a terrible one, and I tried to put it from my mind. I hoped that Zig Zag Road was yesterday's nightmare.

But I had left Wesley trapped in that nightmare ...

Cherokee leaned over, 'What are you thinking about, Gene?'

'I was thinking about Wesley. He's not such a drip.'

Grampa nodded. 'Somebody's growing up,' he said.

I smiled in agreement and then realised that he'd meant me, not Wes.

I hesitated. The beach hut no longer existed, so I

could tell Cherokee about Wesley's secret.

'He's learning to play the clarinet, Grampa.'

'What! Wesley?' Grampa looked surprised and pleased.

'He listens to your music.'

'At 17 Zig Zag Road? I thought music was banned there?'

'It is, but he had a secret place – until Moan found it and smashed everything.'

Cherokee looked horrified. I was going to tell him more but he held up his hand.

'Not another word. This is a problem for Moan, er, I mean, Joan and Wesley. They must sort it out.'

When we arrived at the ferry terminal in Holyhead, there was a long queue of cars and lots of police about. Three plain-clothes detectives were questioning the people in the cars.

'Special Branch,' Grampa muttered. Paddy nodded.

The uniformed police watched as each vehicle was checked. 'That's the back-up in case anyone gets awkward,' Dave told me. I was beginning to get nervous. Had Mrs Walmsley contacted the Welsh police to prevent me leaving the country?

I could only remember having trouble at a Customs

point once before. It was when we were entering the United States of America. Everyone has to fill in a form. One question on it asked something like, 'Do you intend to overthrow the Government of the United States of America?'

Red thought that this was such a daft question that he answered, 'Yes – this is my only reason for visiting your country.' The next moment he was being led into an interrogation room where he was questioned by the FBI for two hours. His nickname didn't help. The FBI officers couldn't believe that George Armstrong had become 'Red' because of the colour of his hair, since Red was now totally bald. To them Red was the colour of his politics!

We would have missed the first concert of the American tour if one Customs official hadn't been a Calumets fan. He recognised Red and persuaded the FBI men that he was famous for his sense of humour. 'And no one could play double bass as brilliantly as he can *and* plan a revolution,' he added and the Calumets hurried away while the FBI were still thinking about that ...

I was wishing that I could hurry away now as the three Special Branch detectives approached the Calumets' Ford Transit van. One of them peered in. He glanced from Paddy to Grampa, then looked at Joe, Dave, Red and me in the back. He smiled slightly, nodded and turned away.

'Must be the fall-out from that bombing in London,' Dave remarked to Joe.

I breathed a sigh of relief. But I was baffled. Surely my oh-so-responsible Aunt Joan would have contacted the authorities as soon as I'd left the house. Why hadn't she?

CHAPTER NINETEEN

Ireland

We drove off the ferry into Dun Laoghaire in a slow-moving column of cars. I stared out of the van window, trying to remember the town.

'Can we park in Dun Laoghaire Shopping Centre?' I asked.

'Why?'

'I want to buy a book.'

'What?' asked Red, brightening up a bit. He was always reading. If I ever complained about having nothing to do, he'd thrust a book into my hands, usually something like *War and Peace*.

'Not a book to read,' I answered, 'a book to write

in.' I knew I'd have time when we got to the hotel to write my diary.

Red guessed what the book was for. 'You writing a diary? I tried that once, but I found I ended up writing about the way I wanted the day to have gone, not the way it had. I couldn't tell the truth ...'

'We've noticed!' came the chorus from everyone but Cherokee.

He was busy thinking about preparations for the Calumets' first concert. Cherokee and Paddy never leave any of the arrangements to chance. Everything – the acoustics, the instruments, the stage – is checked and double checked and over the years they've taught me to help with all this.

I've always been proud of the professional way the Calumets perform. They don't just shamble onto the stage, start tuning up and eventually begin to play after a long chat about what number to do first. That's good enough for amateurs, but not for them.

Joe, Dave and Red walk on stage first and then Grampa comes on. There's a burst of applause, he clicks his fingers in time to their first tune, taps his left foot and they're playing 'Cherokee'. It's as slick a performance as you're ever likely to see.

We stopped for my diary. Red bought something

too – *German is Fun!*

Then we headed for Ernie's in Donnybrook. It was Cherokee's favourite restaurant – and mine too. They have a photo of Cherokee up on the wall. It's in black and white, taken about forty years ago with 'All the best! Cherokee Crawford' scrawled across it in his wild handwriting. It's next to a photo of Robert Mitchum, taken when he was young too, before he had a face like a tortoise.

Red started leafing through *German is Fun!* as we waited for the food to arrive. He didn't seem convinced by the title. 'Mark Twain said a German sense of humour is no laughing matter,' he told me.

I guessed the German lessons wouldn't last long and that I'd never get to meet Red's *fraulein.*

Ten minutes after leaving Ernie's we were at the Shelbourne Hotel in the centre of Dublin. Paddy volunteered to take me on a sightseeing tour of the city while the Calumets were practising that morning. We saw the house of the man who wrote the Dracula stories, and walked down the street where the Duke of Wellington had been born.

'There's a statue of Molly Malone at the top of Grafton Street now. You've heard of her in the old song, I expect.'

Of course, Paddy couldn't resist singing it to me.

> As she wheeled her wheel-barrow
> Through streets broad and narrow
> Crying cockles and mussels, alive alive-o ...

I was just recovering when, walking down Grafton Street, we saw a man made up to look like that famous picture, 'The Mona Lisa' (I saw the real painting when we were in Paris). This man was walking along very slowly, holding a frame around his face. When I pointed at him, he suddenly winked at me!

We were laughing about this as we walked back towards the hotel. I rushed round the large revolving doors first, and held them still so that Paddy was stuck inside. He made weird faces at me through the glass while he pushed. I made faces back then let go of the door without warning. As I expected, Paddy shot out at great speed. What I hadn't planned on was that he would crash into a figure who'd been standing in the shadows of the hotel foyer.

It was like a giraffe charging a rhino. I mean, you wouldn't worry about the rhino getting hurt, would you? The woman didn't so much fall over as roll on her side when Paddy was flung against her.

He leapt up muttering apologies. 'Lord help us! So

sorry, missus. My fault, my fault. Are you hurt now?'

She brushed him aside and glared at me. I stared in disbelief.

It was Moan!

CHAPTER TWENTY

Showdown

Moan and I confronted each other.

'So this is where you're staying,' she commented, surveying the grand old hotel without interest.

I just nodded. The sight of Moan in such unfamiliar surroundings was weird. And there was something different about her. Out of her own house, she seemed smaller, more vulnerable.

'Where's Wesley?' I asked.

'He's quite all right,' she answered defensively, as if reading my suspicious thoughts. 'He's here with me. He's been up to your room to find you.'

Good old Wes, I thought, trying to give me advance warning.

I gave Moan a sort of half smile. 'I'll go and find him,' I said, and before she could point out that he was bound to return, I raced away. I couldn't talk to her yet. I needed to see Wes first.

I found him standing outside my door.

'Wes!' I cried, charging along the corridor towards him. I didn't know which question to ask first: How did you get here? How did you get Moan to come? What happened after I left?

But when I saw my two abandoned diaries in Wesley's hands, I was silent.

'Come on in,' I said, unlocking the door.

He looked around the room, then sank into a chair.

'Thanks for planning my escape,' I blurted out. 'Another week and I would've started tunnelling!'

'That's okay. That was the fun bit. What followed wasn't so cosy. We had one hell of an argument after you left.'

I remembered Moan was still down in the foyer. I'd done just what I disliked Cherokee doing – I'd escaped from trouble. 'Er – shouldn't we get back to Aunt Joan?'

Wes managed a grin. 'Don't worry, she's not a danger

to the public. She's okay down there for a few minutes.'

That reminded me of my diaries. If he'd read them he knew I'd accused Moan of being a homicidal maniac!

'Er – I'll take those,' I said, reaching out for the books.

'If you like,' he said. 'I've read them now.' My heart sank.

'I thought you said people shouldn't read private diaries.' It was the only defence I could think of.

'I figured if you hadn't wanted us to go on reading them you wouldn't have left them,' Wes replied.

I was searching for an answer when the phone rang. I picked it up. 'There's a lady down at reception asking for us. Come on, you can tell me what happened as we go.'

We went downstairs. 'So what did you argue about?' I asked.

'Everything! Going back ten years to when she wouldn't let me be in the Nativity Play in school.'

'Bit late to bring that up now,' I commented as we reached the bottom of the stairs, but I could tell what had happened – the worm had turned. Wesley had had enough of Moan telling him what to do, he'd done some telling back!

I clapped him on the back. 'You gave it to her straight. Good for you!'

'Well ... I made it clear that I wasn't going to give up music and that I didn't feel guilty about your getaway.'

We were standing at the bottom of the stairs. I could see Moan seated in a corner staring grimly ahead.

'Come on. Let's get it over with.' I said, heading towards her.

'Hang on.' Wes held me by the arm. 'I've made some progress, but ... be tactful.'

'When,' I asked, 'am I ever anything else?'

'When you've been scrubbing pots?' Wesley suggested under his breath as we sat down.

Moan sat with her handbag parked on her lap, looking vague and ill at ease. She searched for a familiar subject.

'Nice room?' she asked.

I nodded.

'We're staying down the road,' she informed me. She sniffed. 'Our room's not been cleaned very thoroughly.'

'Some hotels are like that,' I answered, wishing she'd get round to what she really had to say.

There was a long, uncomfortable silence.

'Go on, Mum, tell him,' Wes prompted.

Moan hesitated. 'I'm sorry about what happened,' she rushed out.

'Me too,' I said.

Then, 'I *did* go to the beach hut,' she admitted. 'And I did ...' But her speech came to a halt. Wesley must have already got this confession out of her. And she'd probably promised to admit what she'd done, but now the crunch had come, she couldn't do it.

'Go on, Mum,' Wesley urged. I was finding the silence unbearable and was about to say something, anything, to break it, when Moan began again.

'I *did* open up the beach hut,' she said.

'*Open up!*' She must have wrenched the lock off using a crowbar in those huge hands. It was a bit like Saddam Hussein saying he'd just 'popped in' to Kuwait!

Wes shot me a look that warned me not to say anything.

'I was determined to see what you two had been up to,' Moan dragged out. 'At first I was very angry when I saw all those ... musical things. I'd suspected it, but to see it all!'

Since when has it been a crime to like music? I

wanted to ask, but I didn't. I realised that something had changed between Moan and me. Maybe something had changed her; maybe I was the one who'd changed. Anyway, I couldn't do battle with her any more. It wasn't fair to Wes. And, for the first time, I was beginning to imagine what the situation was like from her point of view. And I started to mumble words I thought I'd never speak.

'Well, it's understandable you not liking music much,' I said. 'After all, you're the one who's had the boring time – staying at home. While your dad, then my dad, went out, having fun, getting famous!'

'Hearing about it all,' Moan added, taking up the thread of what I'd said. 'First, Mother being so angry, telling us music was bad, musicians were irresponsible. Then Clive's death! Music always seemed to be the threat, the enemy.' She turned to me. 'But I didn't damage your clarinet, Gene, or Wesley's records, or whatever they're called.'

'So who did?'

'It was young Mickey,' Wes explained. 'Remember him? Bit slow, hands like an orang-utang. He'd seen us going into the beach hut a few times. When he found it open, he looked in out of curiosity – started fiddling with the tapes. Then he panicked. He's been

in trouble with the Law already. He smashed everything he could lay his hands on.'

Even though the damage was the same, I was
relieved it was some screwed-up kid who'd done it,
not Moan.

'Right,' I said slowly, after a long pause. Moan
wasn't guilty, but she wasn't exactly innocent either.
She had broken in and left it unlocked. She'd been
sneaky and she knew it. More than that, she knew *we*
knew it. Perhaps that was what made her seem different. She'd had to face the fact that we knew she'd
done something wrong.

I'd always hated the way Moan went on and on
about something even after you'd apologised, so now
I was making a huge effort to be more generous than
she'd ever been.

I managed, 'Well, if you're sorry ...'

Clearly Wesley had rehearsed this bit with Moan.
He prompted her. 'Yes. Mum is sorry for what happened. Mum?'

'I'm sorry, very sorry,' said Moan, with a sort of
gulp, but at least she'd said it.

This is revenge! I thought. But why didn't it feel
better?

Then it was my turn.

'And if,' I said, '*if* I've done anything, well, to apologise for ... I ... apologise.'

'Accepted,' said Wes immediately.

'Accepted,' agreed Moan. The Shelbourne sofa gave a soft sigh of relief as she lifted her weight off it. I pretended I hadn't noticed.

'There's a lot of shops back there,' Moan said, pointing towards Grafton Street. I nodded.

'Would any of them sell records?'

Wes and I grinned at each other. Here was Moan wondering whether records had reached Ireland yet. Who was going to explain cassettes and CDs to her?

'Yes,' said Wes, 'only they make little ones now, called CDs.' He wasn't called 'Professor' for nothing!

'Well, let's go and see if we can find some seedies to replace the music you lost,' offered Moan.

Wes and Moan left through the revolving doors, leaving me trying to picture my aunt entering the alien world of HMV!

I felt I needed to think things out, so I went to my room and got out my new diary.

DIARY B

> July 17th, Saturday
> (boiling)

> It was weird seeing Moan here in Dublin. I'd expected her to follow me to the ferry, but I never thought she'd come all this way. And then apologise!

> Now I know why she didn't contact the authorities when I left. She had a guilty conscience about the beach hut and probably thought they'd ask questions if she told them I'd run away from Zig Zag Road. But she's changed and she did say sorry!

> And Wes? He's definitely no pushover any more.

I stopped. My relationship with Moan had moved on and somehow that had altered my view of Cherokee.

I started writing again.

> Cherokee's full of stories about musicians, like Fats Waller and Benny Goodman. He can take hours telling the story of how Clarence 'Pinetop' Smith was shot dead during a fight in a dance hall in Chicago when he was playing the piano. Johnny Hodges, the

saxophonist, died at the dentist. You should
hear Cherokee tell that story! And how about
Charlie Green who died of cold because he
couldn't get into his own house! But he'd never
told me how he'd treated his own family.

I stopped writing and started to think. Whose fault
was it that his daughter had a compulsion about
cleaning? Who'd made her life so shambolic that
she'd had to spend all her time tidying everything?

And what about helping me run away from Zig Zag
Road? No wonder he'd never said an unkind word to
anyone – he'd never stayed around long enough!

I pictured that world-famous smile. Hell, if he was
sincere he'd stop grinning sometimes.

I threw down my pen. I'd given up arguments with
Moan – now I was going to have one with Cherokee!

CHAPTER TWENTY-ONE

The Fall of a Hero

I made my way to the mirrored ballroom where the band was due to play that night. Paddy was already there, having slunk away when Moan appeared.

'Trouble?' he asked.

I couldn't answer him. I asked, 'Where's Cherokee?'

'Not here yet,' said Paddy.

I hung about on the stage. Red's double bass was already propped up there and so were Cherokee's saxophones. I picked up the alto sax. Paddy looked surprised but said nothing. A saxophone is a lovely object. The shape is beautiful and this one was worth thousands of euro. A picture of my mangled clarinet came into my mind and I gripped the saxophone tightly as I thought about Cherokee.

I put the saxophone mouthpiece to my lips and began playing a number that I'd played hundreds of times on the clarinet. It was called 'Stealing Apples'. As I played, my confusion and anger left me and I became absorbed in what I was doing. I knew that I had played well, better than on the clarinet. When I'd finished I held the saxophone gratefully for a moment before replacing it carefully on its stand.

From the far side of the ballroom came the sound of someone clapping. It was Cherokee. He came towards me.

'That was excellent. You should keep on with the saxophone, Gene. One day you'll be very good. Very good.'

That was praise indeed from him. He'd never say anything about music just to be nice. But that irritated me now.

'I don't know whether I'll bother,' I said sulkily.

'Oh, why not?'

'Well, it's not that important is it? Music, I mean.' I looked at him hard. 'There are more important things, like families, for example.'

He didn't seem surprised. 'Yes, Gene, you're right,' he said sadly. 'Look, this is hard to explain. Pick up the saxophone again for a minute.'

'I don't want to play now,' I said firmly.

'I know you don't.' But he took up his saxophone and handed it to me. 'Just play "Edelweiss" will you?'

The temptation to play again was just too great. I took it and began to play.

When I'd finished, Cherokee didn't offer any praise, instead he said, 'Remember when I taught you about "occasional notes"?'

I nodded. 'A piece of music in C can use notes which are not in the scale of C. They're called passing notes.'

'Exactly. They're temporary and don't affect the overall key. On the other hand ...' He took his saxophone and played for about thirty seconds. It was awful! He was in no key at all, just playing random notes.

He put down the saxophone. 'It's the same with a family,' he said. 'Everyone has "occasional notes" – an argument or disagreement here and there, but it doesn't stop them being a family. With your grandmother and me, there weren't just "occasional notes". There was no tune at all. So – it seemed better to part.'

'You abandoned my father!'

'"Abandoned" makes it sound pretty rotten, Gene. I left Clive with his mother who was a very careful and efficient housewife. I sent her money, but I thought it was better not to visit.'

'So when did you see my father again?'

'I thought it was a miracle at the time, but I suppose it would be more accurate to say it was heredity at work. Clive grew up loving music, despite his mother's discouragement. When he was fifteen, he searched me out, travelled all the way to Manchester, where I was playing, to find me ...'

'What happened then?'

'He'd never had an opportunity before to try playing the drums. But when he began, it was obvious that he had real talent and he just refused to return home. From then on he stayed with me. Your grandmother never forgave me and your aunt thought I'd robbed her of a brother.'

'So that's why she's always insisted that I visit her. I've been a substitute.'

'And a good one, Gene. Don't underestimate how much pleasure your visits have given your aunt.'

I blushed with shame.

'I think we'd all have been friends again if Clive had

lived,' Cherokee continued. 'Joan and her mother would eventually have realised that music made him happy.'

I didn't know what to say. I'd hate to have a son and see him die before me. That's worse than being an orphan, as I am. I stared at Cherokee, not knowing how to break the silence. But then Paddy did it for me.

'Look who's blown in!' he called out. It was my good friend Seamus!

Cherokee and I were both glad to give our attention to someone else.

'Seamus!' I said. 'How did you get here?' I hadn't expected to see him until we reached Kerry.

'My dad was going to Limerick, and I hitched a lift the rest of the way,' he explained.

'Glad to see you, lad,' Cherokee added warmly. Of course Seamus was a favourite – wasn't he good at music? My unresolved argument with Cherokee hung in the air.

'P'raps we'll go out for a bit,' I said, not looking directly at him.

Cherokee understood. 'Of course, of course.'

Seamus was standing with his rucksack hanging by his side. He looked hot, just like someone who'd hitched half-way across Ireland on a warm summer's afternoon.

'Thirsty?' I asked.

Seamus started panting as an answer. 'Come on, let's find somewhere to have a cool drink,' I said, edging him away.

'Need any money?' asked Cherokee, automatically putting his hand in his pocket.

'We'll manage,' I answered and half pushed Seamus towards the ballroom exit.

CHAPTER TWENTY-TWO

But on the Third Day...

'What's up?' Seamus asked as soon as we were outside in the crowds around St Stephen's Green.

That's the great thing about our friendship. We don't see each other for months, years even, but we don't go through a polite distant phase. No chat about the fine weather we're having from Seamus!

So I answered just as directly. 'Cherokee never told me the truth about the way he treated his family,' I said, as we joined a queue at an ice-cream kiosk.

'You mean he lied?'

'No. Er – do you want vanilla? Two vanilla

ice-creams please – big.'

I was beginning to feel that the drama of the situation was ebbing away. As Seamus and I ambled into St Stephen's Green I tried to recall my strong sense of betrayal at learning – what? That Cherokee hadn't been a perfect father to Moan? I'd already guessed that from her attitude towards him. That Cherokee hadn't stayed home and looked after a little child? I'd always known he hadn't done that – even for me!

'I suppose,' I explained slowly, 'I've just realised that Cherokee isn't perfect.'

Seamus stopped still, his mouth open and his tongue white from the ice-cream.

Then he said, 'Jesus, Gene, aren't you learning that all the time?'

I laughed, some of the tension evaporating. Seamus started to elaborate. He had a long list of people he'd realised weren't perfect. 'Sure, if I thought anyone was perfect it would be Cherokee,' he went on. 'Uncle Paddy being his road manager makes him near perfect in Kerry – specially since he did that ad. They play that on RTE nearly every night – but nobody's perfect.'

'I suppose so but if ...' I was trying to think of a way

of explaining how my perspective on the world had changed. 'If Cherokee isn't perfect, then Aunt Joan isn't as bad as I thought.'

Seamus knew all about my Aunt Joan. I'd told his entire family about her. His mum had even considered sending me food parcels when she knew I was staying at Zig Zag Road. I'd milked them all for sympathy. Perhaps what I was feeling was guilt for the way I'd behaved. That made me realise how self-centred I was being now.

'How's your mum and dad?' I asked.

'Grand!'

'And your singing?'

'Want to hear?'

'Okay!'

We raced back to the hotel, dodging between people and cars and swung into the Shelbourne again. Paddy was in the foyer. 'Herself's come back,' he announced.

'And Wesley?' I asked.

He nodded 'Your man's here.'

'Good. He'll stick up for me.'

Somewhere in the hotel, Cherokee and Moan were discussing my future. Paddy had told me that back in 1922 the country's new Constitution had been planned in one of the rooms of the Shelbourne Hotel. I bet that occasion was a party compared with these negotiations. Cherokee was doing what I knew was the most difficult thing for him. He was facing a confrontation.

Then an awful idea struck me. I'd made Cherokee feel pretty guilty about the way he'd behaved towards his family. Supposing he'd lost his confidence and decided he wasn't doing a good job of bringing me up? Supposing he thought I'd prefer Zig Zag Road!

I panicked. 'Paddy! Where are Cherokee and the others?'

Paddy hesitated. 'He said they had something to discuss without you.' To Paddy what Cherokee said was the Law.

'Please, Paddy,' I urged, 'tell me where they are.'

'I'll tell you which room they're using if you promise not to go in.'

'What's the good of that? I've got to tell Cherokee I want him to remain my guardian. Please, Paddy, this is life or death!'

Paddy shook his head. 'I'm sorry, Gene, your grandfather said you mustn't go in.'

I tried one last time. 'Is that exactly what he said – that I "mustn't go in"?'

'Exactly.'

'Well then, tell me which room they're all in and I promise not to go in.'

Paddy nodded. 'Okay – Remember now, you've promised. Room 201.'

'Thanks, Paddy! Wait here.' I added to Seamus. Then I grabbed Cherokee's saxophone and headed towards the stairs. I couldn't wait for the lift, but leapt up the stairs three at a time. Carrying the saxophone made it difficult to move fast, but I raced towards Room 201.

I put an ear to the door. Moan's voice. I dreaded to think what she was telling Cherokee about me. I was hoping she wouldn't want him to know about her five minutes of fame on 'Life's a Laf'.

I put the saxophone to my lips and played. I played an old tune called 'I Believe In You' which Cherokee had taught me years before. I hoped he could hear and that he remembered the words.

> I believe in you. I believe in you –
> I hear the sound of good solid judgement
> Whenever you talk ...

I finished. There was silence on the other side of the door. Then it opened.

'Wesley!'

'Gene, you're playing the saxophone!'

I nodded. 'This is the instrument for me,' I said, and I meant it too. Wesley smiled.

'Cherokee's going to buy me a clarinet,' he said. 'He said he's got to buy you a new one too. We'll all go together.'

'Great!' I looked past him to where Moan was sitting. She wasn't smiling, but at least she wasn't scowling either.

'Come on in, Gene.' It was Moan's voice. I edged in. There was a silence that nobody seemed keen to break. Then Wesley asked, 'Will you still give me lessons when you come to stay?'

'When I stay ...?' I trailed off, hardly daring to ask whether I was to be at Zig Zag Road permanently.

'On your holidays,' he added.

'So I'll be staying with Cherokee!' I couldn't keep the relief out of my voice.

Wesley nodded. He had certainly changed. He was not going to be pushed around any longer. There'd be music at 17 Zig Zag Road in the future.

'Seamus is downstairs,' I told Wesley.

He hesitated. 'Come on,' I said encouragingly. 'He's dying to meet you. I've told him all about you.'

CHAPTER TWENTY-THREE

A to Z

Seamus, Wesley and I set up in the ballroom and started to practise. Seamus played the piano as well as he sang, so the three of us made an okay sound. By five o'clock we were discussing what we should name ourselves.

'Something Indian,' suggested Seamus. 'You know, to show we're an off-shoot of the Calumets?' He'd soon got over his reserve with Wes. I hoped he'd forgotten some of the stories I'd told him about my cousin in the past!

We never did resolve the question of a name because Cherokee came in and asked to hear a

number. We stopped larking about. In front of Cherokee we were going to play as well as we could. We
played 'I Know Why', a number we'd practised that
afternoon. Half-way through, when I was waiting to
come in on the saxophone, I looked down at Cherokee. He seemed tinier than ever, perhaps I'd grown
while I'd been at Moan's. He looked older too. My
grandfather, my famous fabulous – but not perfect –
grandfather.

'Excellent,' he said quietly when we'd finished. For
a moment I thought he was upset about something.
There seemed to be tears in his eyes. Then I understood. He came up on stage and put an arm around
Wes and me.

'My two grandsons – playing together,' he said.
'Whoever would have thought it! And with an O'Flaherty too,' he added, smiling at Seamus.

'I've got it!' I cried. 'Our new name – it's got to be
Professor O'Flaherty's Trio!'

'I like the O'Flaherty, but where does the "Professor" bit come in?' asked Seamus.

'That's Wes's nickname,' I explained. 'Because he's
brilliant at school.'

Wesley hung his shoulders and head in
embarrassment.

'Don't be modest,' said Cherokee. 'Performers can't afford too much modesty! Now if you three whizz-kids would kindly leave, we old Calumets need to tune up.'

That evening the members of Professor O'Flaherty's Trio were seated at a table by the stage with Paddy when we were joined by the last person in the world I'd ever expected to see at a musical event – Aunt Joan.

She sat down heavily and gripped her handbag firmly in both hands as if she expected it to be snatched away at any moment. And yet she had travelled to Ireland for me.

During a gap between numbers, I leaned over. 'Er – Auntie – thanks.'

'What for, Gene?'

'For coming here ... I know you didn't want to ... er ... it must have interfered with your spring cleaning.'

Wesley grinned, but Moan seemed to be struggling to say something. 'Well ... it can wait ... I suppose,' she managed. Wesley winked at me. I grinned. I was going to start again with Moan.

And perhaps I wasn't the only one to be starting afresh. As the Calumets started to play 'Take The A Train', I felt my chair begin to shake. The floor seemed to be moving. As the music grew faster so the shaking increased. I looked down and saw the cause – Moan's feet were tapping to the music.

'Still writing your diary?' Red asked me next morning at breakfast.

'Yeah. Still teaching yourself German?'

'*Ya. Ich lerne gerne,*' replied Red and moved off, talking in what I guess was German.

I'd said I was still writing my diary, but later that day when I had time to write, I realised I had a choice to make. I now had three books – the original diaries A and B and the new Diary B. Which should I write in? Eventually I picked up the new book.

DIARY B

This could just as easily be Diary A, because, for the first time since I began, what I'm meant to think and what I do think are the same!

Here, Mrs Walmsley, wherever you are, are my innermost thoughts, if you're still interested, which I doubt, now that Cherokee and Moan have decided to be my joint guardians. And thank you, by the way, for agreeing to this. I suppose it will mean filling out a whole load of official forms!

It was great to have Cousin Wesley and my aunt in the audience last night. Having the family united made Cherokee feel good too, I could tell. He played even better than usual and I felt proud when the audience cheered and yelled at the end of the concert!

At least my aunt's first night away from Zig Zag Road was a memorable one. She and Wesley are now on their way back home. Wes wasn't looking forward to the plane journey. He told me Moan had driven the cabin crew close to madness on the way to Dublin by asking questions about whether the plane was safe, like: 'Are you sure you've closed all the windows?'

'Why don't you take her home by ferry?' I'd suggested. It was like the conversations Red and I had about transporting his double bass.

'No fear,' Wes had replied. 'If the plane crashes, I can't do anything about it, but if the ferry sinks, I'll have to try to save her from drowning!'

I've also, Mrs Walmsley, worked out what 'peer group bonding' is. It's liking people of your own age. Well, I like some, and I know

now that Wesley's been a good friend to me. We had a conversation after the concert that made me think.

I'd said how his waistcoat would look good on stage. He'd replied, 'Thanks. So you like it now then?'

The word 'now' reminded me of some of the jibes I'd written in Diary B.

I started apologising. Luckily he's easy to apologise to. He laughed and said, 'Don't worry. You should read what I wrote about you in my diary. Not that it's as interesting as yours. Ever thought about being a writer?'

I didn't answer. There's two bits to that question and I'm trying to work out whether he meant both of them. The first is obvious. (1) Wes, who's clever, thinks my writing is good enough for me to do it for a living. That's the good news.

Here's the bad: (2) He doesn't take it for granted that I'm going to be a musician. Aren't I good enough? I can't imagine not being part of the musical world. If anyone was born to be part of it, it's me, but perhaps I'm not meant to be a performer. I'm not as single-minded as Cherokee, I know that ...

I'm renaming this Diary C, since it's no longer the diary Mrs Walmsley forced me to write, nor the one I wrote secretly. If this goes on, I shall probably get through the alphabet!

What will Diary Z be like? I'll imagine an extract:

DIARY Z

> (Dry and hotter than the Sahara, thanks to global warming)

I am here at Zig Zag Road, now tottering on the edge of a cliff. Returning to visit Aunt Joan is a great idea when I want a perfectly ironed shirt. Not that we jazz critics are noted for our sharp dressing! My Aunt Joan is a useful person to check my reviews with too. If she can understand them, then so can any reader! She's learnt a lot about music since the bad old days.

Her cooking hasn't improved though. Fortunately I can now afford to take her out to a restaurant. Sometimes Wesley, now better known as 'Professor Lank Crawford', the world famous jazz clarinetist, comes along too. He took our grandfather's surname —

Crawford, when he became a full-time clarinetist. However famous he gets, he knows
he'll never shake off being introduced as, 'Professor Lank Crawford, grandson of the
greatest saxophonist of them all — Cherokee
Crawford!'

He doesn't mind. He says he never plays a
note without thinking of Cherokee. And J
never write a word without thinking of him
either.